LEGO Friends

Showtime!

STORIES • TRIVIA • QUIZZES

Friends forever :)

Ladybird

Published by Ladybird Books Ltd 2013
A Penguin Company
Penguin Books Ltd, 80 Strand, London, WC2R 0RL, UK
Penguin Books Australia Ltd, 707 Collins Street, Melbourne,
Victoria 3008, Australia (a division of Pearson Australia
Group Pty Ltd)

www.ladybird.com

AMEET Produced by AMEET Sp. z o.o.
       under license from the LEGO Group.

AMEET Sp. z o.o.,
Przybyszewskiego 176/178, 93-120 Łódź – Poland
ameet@ameet.com.pl
www.ameet.pl

Penguin Books Ltd, 80 Strand, London, WC2R 0RL, UK
Please keep the Penguin Books Ltd address for future reference.

www.LEGO.com

ISBN: 9780723271215
001 - 10 9 8 7 6 5 4 3 2 1
Printed in Poland

Item name: LEGO® Friends. Showtime!
Series: LNR
Item number: LNR 101/LNR 102
Batch: 01/GB

Welcome!

Welcome to Heartlake City

This beautiful town is located by the side of a heart-shaped lake. It is here that five cool girls live. They met by accident, but became friends straight away. Together, they go on great adventures and have an awesome time. Like all friends, they laugh, share secrets and chat. Maybe you would like to be friends with them too?

Meet the Girls

Olivia is practical and down-to-earth. She's also an out-of-this-world inventor, creating anything and everything from a robot to a waterproof microphone. This is one seriously talented girl.

Olivia

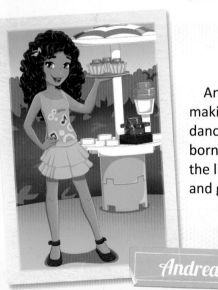

Andrea is a superstar in the making. A fabulous singer, dancer and actress, this girl was born to be on the stage. She's the life and soul of any party and great fun to be around.

Andrea

Stephanie is super-together and always full of ideas. She always keeps everyone on their toes and likes nothing better than throwing amazing – and very organised – parties for her friends.

Stephanie

Emma is totally creative and spends hours experimenting with new looks and styles. She's also got a black belt in karate – but would much prefer it if the belt was the colour pink!

Emma

Mia

Mia likes nothing better than being surrounded by her friends and animals. This girl loves all creatures, whether they're big or small, cuddly or fierce; and they simply adore her right back.

Film Star Fun

The five friends had gathered in their tree house after school, as usual. They were busy catching up with the day's events, while the radio that Olivia had built herself blared out their favourite channel. Andrea was in the middle of telling everyone about her audition for the school play when Stephanie suddenly shushed her.

"Sor-ry!" huffed Andrea.

"Listen a minute," said Stephanie, gesturing towards the radio. "You'll want to hear this!"

The local radio presenter was making an announcement. A film crew would be arriving in Heartlake City the very next day to shoot a documentary about animals!

"Wow!' Andrea exclaimed, reaching for her bag and rooting around for her lip gloss. "Filmmakers! I need to look fabulous – maybe they'll need some extras!"

"Er, it's going to be a documentary about animals," Emma pointed out. "What would you be? A grizzly bear?!"

"Oh," Andrea sighed dramatically. "And here was me thinking it was my chance to be discovered." She struck a pose. "I'm ready for my close-up."

"Shh!" exclaimed Olivia.

"Why is everyone always shushing me?" Andrea exclaimed.

"Look," said Olivia, pointing out of the tree house to where her cat, Kitty, was crouched on the ground, gazing longingly at a bird that had landed next to her.

"Shoo, Kitty !" shouted Mia.

The bird flew into the air, deftly escaping the cat's claws. The bird landed on a surprised Kitty 's head, pecking her with its beak, before flying off again.

The girls giggled.

"Poor old Kitty," laughed Mia. "I'm glad the bird escaped though."

"That's given me an idea," said Stephanie. "Why don't we make our own film about animals? We could make it really funny."

"Brilliant!" exclaimed Mia. "Count me in."

The others nodded in agreement.

Stephanie whipped out her notebook. "Right," she said, licking the top of her pen and making a few notes. "I suggest we film the stables, the veterinary clinic and all of our pets. Let's start at the stables. I'll work out a schedule."

"Good idea," said Olivia. "I'll grab my video and laptop. Let's meet at the stables in half an hour."

As the girls walked into the stables, they spotted one of the grooms they knew, holding a beautiful bouquet of flowers.

"Hi David. What are you up to?" asked Andrea, nodding at Olivia to start filming.

"It's Freya's birthday," he explained. "I've brought her some flowers."

Olivia carried on filming as David strode over to the side of the paddock where Freya was giving a riding lesson, hiding the flowers behind his back. Unfortunately, he didn't notice when Niki, Mia's horse, crept up behind him and started eating the flowers! The girls couldn't help laughing, as Olivia filmed David presenting a confused Freya with a half-eaten bunch of stems. Niki stood by the fence, calmly polishing off her tasty snack, with the last half-chewed flower dangling from her mouth.

Next on the list to be filmed was Andrea's extremely cute pet rabbit, Jazz. Stephanie's pink crab, Crabby, wasn't quite so cute, but the girls had to laugh as he looked straight into the camera, his eyes sticking out on their long stalks.

"It's like he knows he's being filmed!" laughed Emma.

Finally, the filming was complete and the girls grabbed a table outside their local café to admire their masterpiece. The girls couldn't stop giggling as they replayed the film. They laughed so hard that Marie, the owner of the café, came over to see what was going on, together with a large man dressed in a very expensive suit.

Rabbit

Crab

On the screen they could see Emma practising her horse jumping. She was so busy waving at the camera that she didn't notice one of the obstacles. But the horse did, and came to a screeching halt. Emma flew out of the saddle and turned a perfect somersault in the air, before landing upside down in a haystack. The horse looked surprised for a moment, then calmly started munching on one of Emma's boots.

Everyone burst out laughing.

"Beautiful somersault, Em!" said Mia.

"Let's see the scenes from the clinic," said Stephanie.

The girls had filmed this clip in the morning. A woman arrived at the veterinary clinic with an adorable baby chimpanzee from the local zoo. As the vet and the woman were chatting away, the chimp had suddenly disappeared without a trace. Everyone ran around frantically looking for it, until finally Olivia's camera captured a brown paw throwing a banana skin out of the rubbish bin. Mia rushed over to grab the chimp, but slipped on the banana skin. She skidded backwards, landing in a heap on top of Aunt Sophie, the owner of the clinic. The chimp leapt out of the bin, whooping and clapping with delight at the chaos he had caused.

Emma's legs :)

"Brilliant," said the man in the suit, wiping tears of laughter from his eyes. "My crew could learn a thing or two from you, girls." He grinned around the table. "I'm a director. We're currently making a documentary about all the animals in Heartlake City."

The friends looked at each other excitedly. The director glanced over their shoulders, and suddenly his expression changed.

Oops!

"Thomas!" the director shouted, making the girls jump. "What happened?"

The girls looked round to see an upset-looking man, clutching something in his hands. Something that looked remarkably like . . .

"Is that film reel?" Olivia asked. "Oh, no!"

"It's not my fault," the cameraman sighed in despair. "I was editing the material, when this cat appeared out of nowhere. Before I could stop him, he had managed to pull all the film out of the cartridge. It's ruined." He handed the tangled mess to the director.

"But we don't have time to reshoot!" the director moaned, as he held up the pieces of exposed and chewed-up film. "We're due at the studio with complete footage of the animals, first thing tomorrow!"

The girls stared at each other in horror. For a moment, everything seemed lost, but then the director's eye fell on Olivia's laptop.

"Unless . . ." he began, his face suddenly lighting up. "Unless you girls can help?"

"Us?" Emma sat up straight and started smoothing her hair. "How?"

"Your video," the director explained. "Let us use it. Your footage is great, so natural and really funny. The audience will love it."

"Are you serious?" Stephanie gulped.

"Absolutely," the director replied happily. "We'll just shoot a few more scenes together, then edit it. What do you say?"

"We're in!" shouted Andrea, jumping up and giving the director a hug.

A moment later, the director and the cameraman were discussing the details excitedly. The girls grinned happily at each other.

"See," grinned Andrea. "I said I was ready for my close-up."

"Shh!" laughed the others.

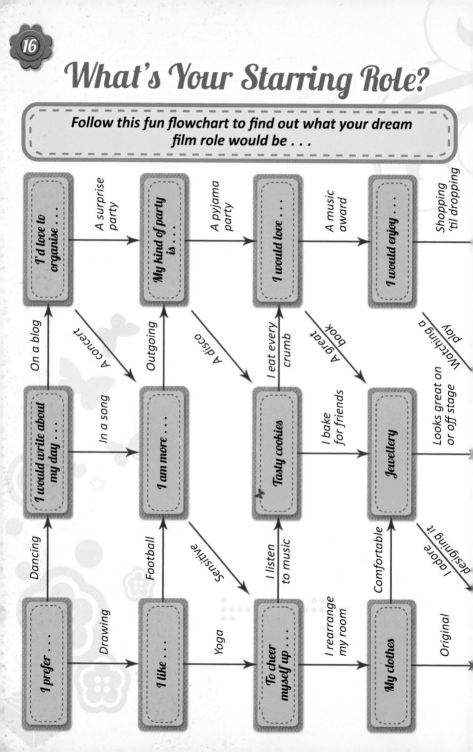

Star

You're the life and soul of every party and love nothing better than being the centre of attention. You were born to be on the stage, dah-ling.

Writer

You prefer to be behind the scenes rather than in the spotlight. You love losing yourself in a great book or fab film. You'd make a fantastic script writer.

Designer

You love to stand out from the crowd in eye-catching clothes, and turn heads wherever you go. You'd wow everyone as a stylist or costume designer.

Camera vs Microphone

Andrea has always dreamed of being a pop star, but she thinks being an actress would be pretty amazing too. Read on to decide what you think she should be.

If I was a famous singer:

- Fans all over the world would want my autograph.

- Teenagers would cover their bedroom walls with posters of me!

- I'd record the best album in the world. Everyone would love it.

- I'd go on a sell-out world tour.

- I'd be number one in the charts.

If I became an actress:

- I'd be able to play a different character every single day.

- I'd have my own dressing-room.

- I'd be given award after award.

- Every chat show would want to interview me.

- I'd have lots of famous friends.

Friendship Predictor

Do this fun quiz with a friend. Take it in turns to read the questions and circle the statements that most apply to each of you. Simply find the symbol each of you chose the most on the Friendship Table. The place where both your icons meet reveals the prediction for your friendship . . .

My personality:
- ♡ I'm pretty stubborn.
- ♪ I love being the centre of attention.
- ☆ My head is always in the clouds.
- ✿ I can be a bit, er, OK, a lot, bossy.
- 🐾 I always speak my mind.

My spare time:
- ♡ I love sports.
- ♪ The world is my catwalk.
- ☆ Clumsy is my middle name.
- ✿ Being organised is super-important.
- 🐾 I always put my foot in it.

My dream job:
- ♡ I'd like to work in a modern laboratory.
- ♪ I'd be happiest designing super-stylish outfits.
- ☆ I'd love to be a top journalist.
- ✿ I want to be famous.
- 🐾 Working with animals would be my dream.

My passions:

- ♡ Learning new things rocks my world.
- ♪ Dancing and singing are my life.
- ☆ I'm great at making up stories.
- ❀ I love being on stage.
- ❀ I'm great at getting things done.

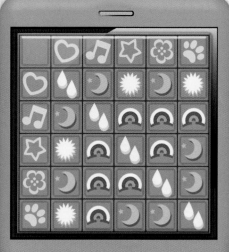

You two were made for each other. You love the same stuff and enjoy doing the same things. In fact, you didn't need to take this test to know that, did you?

At first glance, you don't seem to have much in common. But it doesn't matter as you both really like each other. After all, opposites attract, you know.

You guys are a pretty good match. It's certainly no surprise that you two are friends. You're a good team, and will always be there for each other.

You aren't the best match in the world, but who said you had to be? If you both work at your friendship, you can have a fab time together.

The Mysterious Owner

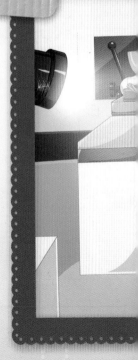

Mia was the last of the five friends to reach the café. She'd had to work late at the veterinary clinic and night was already drawing in.

All of the customers had stopped what they were doing to watch Andrea singing one of her favourite songs.

All except one woman, who was sitting alone in the corner, busily scribbling something on a napkin. As soon as her set was over, Andrea rushed over to her friends.

"You were great!" cried Emma, flinging her arms around Andrea's neck, accidentally knocking over a vase of flowers at the same time.

"Amazing," Stephanie agreed, winking at Andrea, as Emma picked up the flowers. "It won't be long until I'm managing your sell-out world tour!"

"Let's just hope there aren't too many vases in your dressing room for me to knock over," laughed Emma.

The girls decided to head to their tree house, as soon as Andrea finished her shift. Andrea finished her work as fast as she could. Just as they were leaving, Andrea noticed a crumpled up napkin on one of the tables. She quickly shoved it into her back pocket and ran to catch up with her friends.

The girls were busy discussing the big news of the day. A mysterious buyer had bought the Heartlake stables and horses. No one knew the new owner's identity, as the whole deal had been arranged by a butler.

"I don't like it," Stephanie said ominously, looking up from the latest book in the series about the wizard Chiara. It was written by her favourite author, Fox. "How do we know the new owner will take good care of the horses?"

"Who will give them lumps of sugar? Or cover them with blankets at night?" asked Andrea.

"And ribbons," added Emma. "Don't forget about the ribbons in their manes."

"But why hide their identity like that?" Andrea asked. She started searching in her pocket. "Achoo!" she sneezed.

"Bless you," said Emma.

But Andrea wasn't listening. She was looking at the crumpled napkin that she'd pulled out of her pocket while trying to find a tissue. "What's this?" she asked, puzzled. "It's got scribbles all over it."

"Ooh, show us!" Stephanie said excitedly. "Maybe it's a love letter one of the customers wrote for you!"

Intrigued, the girls gathered to look at the napkin. There were just a few words written on it:

Stable? Horses? New chapter! Chiara and the magic horse? Think about it!!!

"Chiara and the magic horse," Andrea read out loud.

"Well, it's definitely not a love letter," sighed Emma.

"Hang on," said Mia, thinking. "That woman in the café was scribbling on a napkin. This must be hers. So does she have something to do with the stables, do you think?"

"And with Fox's books," Stephanie added, waving her book excitedly. "A new chapter . . . Chiara . . . It all fits."

"Maybe she's Fox's secretary?" Emma said.

"We've got to find out who the owner is," Olivia said. "And find the woman who wrote this. Everything's connected somehow. I just don't know how yet . . . We need to find the butler. Only he can tell us who the owner is."

The next day, the girls did their best to track down
the mysterious butler. They found out three things. Firstly, the
butler always travelled in a black limousine. Secondly, he often
popped into the post office to either post or pick up very thick
envelopes. And thirdly, he had been spotted in the bakery
and the grocers, but after that the trail went cold. The
girls were no nearer to finding out the identity of
the mysterious new owner, or who
the woman in the café was.

Mia had to leave to take her beautiful white horse, Robin, out for a ride.

"Maybe I'll see the new owner," she said.

But to her disappointment there was no sign of the mysterious buyer at the stables. "Never mind, Robin," she whispered to her horse, as they trotted out of the yard. "Whatever happens, I'll make sure the new owner takes care of you."

Just then, she spotted another horse rider in the distance – and she looked just like the woman from the café!

"Excuse me," she called.

The woman glanced over, then pulled on her horse's reins and rode away.

"Come on, Robin!" Mia cried. "She's not getting away that easily!"

Robin broke into a gallop and the pair gave chase along the old railway tracks and out on to Rockwood Lane, almost colliding with Stephanie and Emma.

"Whoa!" shouted Mia, pulling back on Robin's reins.

"Whoa, is right," tutted Emma, smoothing down her hair. "First that woman nearly rode right over us, and now you . . ."

"You saw her!" exclaimed Mia. "That's the woman from the café! Quick! Which way did she go?"

Stephanie pointed towards the end of the street. "That way. But you'll never catch up with her now."

"Oh," sighed Mia, dismounting. "There goes our only hope of getting some answers."

Stephanie grinned at her friend. "Ah, but that's where you're wrong," she said. "I searched online to find out if any large houses have been sold near the stables recently. After all, the new owner has to live somewhere and I don't think they're going to move into one of the empty horse stalls, do you?"

"Pretty clever, huh?" said Emma, as proud as if it was her own idea.

"And . . ." Stephanie said, "it turns out the only property that has been sold recently is the old house at
13 Rockwood Lane."

Just then the girls spotted Olivia and Andrea, who were being pulled towards them by Coco – one of the smartest dogs they knew.

"The butler dropped a handkerchief outside the bakery," panted Olivia, clutching on to Coco's lead. "I thought Coco's sense of smell could track the butler down."

"Everything fits . . ." nodded Stephanie. She quickly filled Olivia and Andrea in. "The writer's secretary arrived here on horseback. The butler's trail also leads to Rockwood Lane and we know that someone has bought a house on this street."

"So what do we do now?" asked Emma, uncertainly.

"We knock on the door and greet the owner of course!" smiled Olivia. "Isn't that how the people of Heartlake City always welcome their new neighbours?"

She turned towards Number 13. "Come on, girls!"

"I think I'm a little bit scared," Andrea whispered, holding tightly on to Coco's lead.

"Look!" Olivia pointed at a black limousine parked in the driveway. "It's the butler's car."

She marched up to the front door and knocked loudly. But no one answered.

"Perhaps they're in the garden?" suggested Mia. The girls walked round the side of the house. No one was in the garden, but the patio doors leading onto the terrace were open.

"Hello?" called Mia, "Is anybody home?"

"Come in," shouted a voice, from deep inside the house. "I'll be with you in a minute." The girls hesitated for a moment, then cautiously stepped inside.

They found themselves inside a large room, with a huge comfy-looking sofa and two armchairs on either side of the fireplace. In the corner was a desk with a laptop surrounded by piles of books.

"I'd know those anywhere!" exclaimed Stephanie. "That's every single book in the Chiara series." She hurried over for a closer look. Andrea followed behind her, accidentally brushing against the laptop. Its screen burst into life. Stephanie caught her breath. "No way!" she gasped, clutching her chest and pointing at the screen.

Andrea peered over her shoulder. "Chiara in the Land of Darkness, by Fox," she read out loud.

"There's no such book in the series," Stephanie whispered, her eyes wide. "At least, not yet!"

Olivia hurried over. "Look," she said, pointing at an envelope on the table. "That letter's addressed to Fox. This is where the writer lives!"

"What are you doing here?"

The girls nearly jumped out of their skin as they suddenly heard a woman's voice behind them. Turning, the girls saw the woman from the café, still dressed in riding gear. She didn't look happy. "Who are you? I was expecting a delivery from the antique shop."

Mia stepped forward. "We're so sorry. We did knock, and you told us to come in. We came to meet the new owner of the stables. You see, we really love the horses . . ."

". . . But then we couldn't help but notice the laptop and the envelope!" Stephanie interrupted. "Does Fox really live here? Sorry," she said quickly as the woman looked taken aback. "We honestly didn't mean to pry. I noticed the books and went for a closer look, then Andrea accidentally knocked the laptop and we saw what was on the screen. Then we noticed the letter addressed to Fox."

"Everyone in Heartlake City would be so excited to have a famous writer living here," added Andrea. Mia and Emma nodded enthusiastically.

The woman coolly examined them.

"All right," she said slowly. "I can see I'm not going to be able to hide anything from you."

"Does that mean you'll let us meet Fox?" asked Stephanie excitedly. "And ask for his autograph?"

"If you promise not to tell anyone . . ." the woman looked searchingly at the girls.

"Word of honour!" they cried together.

The woman nodded. "It seems I have no choice. But sit down first, you're making me nervous."

Looking at each other excitedly, the girls hurried to the sofa, while the woman sat in one of the armchairs. She took a deep breath.

"My name is Marcia Bowman. But you'd know me better as Fox."

"But–" interrupted Olivia.

Marcia held up her hand. "Yes, you thought Fox was a man. Everyone does. But it's my pen name. I prefer to be anonymous.

That way, I can get on with what I do best: writing."

She smiled at the girls' shocked faces. "What would you all say to a cup of tea? You look as though you could do with it."

"That's . . ." Olivia began slowly.

". . . Ab-so-lutely fantastic!" Emma squealed.

Marcia looked at them all, as her butler served tea. "I have an idea," she said. "What if I included you in my new book?"

"Who?" said Andrea, almost dropping her tea cup. "Us?"

"Yes, you!" Marcia smiled. "I would have to get to know you all better first. It would really help."

"W-w-w-we . . ." gasped Stephanie, hardly able to speak.

Marcia looked amused. "Unless you don't want me to, of course."

The girls' excited screams could probably be heard all over Heartlake City.

Reading fun

Over the next few days, the girls showed Marcia all round Heartlake City. They visited Lighthouse Island, Makepeace Castle and the stables. But they didn't reveal to anyone who their new companion really was.

Finally the new novel by Fox appeared in the shops. The friends met in the tree house and excitedly started to read the book out loud.

"... and then Chiara met five new wizards," Stephanie read. The girls grinned at each other. "Chiara knew immediately that they'd be friends, because they laughed a lot – just like her. Each girl had her own special power. The first one could create amazing pictures. The second could speak to all the animals. The third could weave magic with her beautiful singing voice. Whatever the fourth one wrote came true. And the last one could create constructions that were beyond even your wildest dreams."

"Well," Emma winked at her friends. "They certainly sound a little familiar. I can't believe we're actually in one of Fox's books."

"One thing's for sure," laughed Stephanie. "This is one story you really couldn't make up!"

Horsing Around

The friends spend a lot of their time helping to look after the horses at the stables. Here are some fascinating horse facts they have prepared, just for you . . .

Happy birthday!

The average length of a horse's life is 25 years, but the oldest horse ever lived to 62!

Smile, please!

Newborn foals have just four teeth, but an adult horse has between 30 and 40. It is actually possible to estimate a horse's age by examining its teeth.

Hair care

Do you and your friends ever exchange friendly nudges? Horses do the same, but they do it by lightly nibbling each other. This helps them to take care of each other's hair and skin.

Little and large

The smallest horse in the world was less than half a metre tall! The biggest horse known was five times taller than that, and weighed 1,500 kg (the same as a minibus for a whole family!).

Goodnight!

Horses can sleep standing up, but also enjoy lying down, just like us. Most horses need no more than around three hours of sleep a day.

Writers' Tips

Marcia Bowman definitely knows how to write a great novel. Here are her tips on how to become a writer . . .

Be like a detective – watch, listen, look around. Lots of things happen around you, and you can write about them.

Think of a great title. Make sure it really catches the reader's imagination.

Don't forget to show someone your work. Keeping it in a drawer won't make you a bestselling author!

Think about how you can surprise your reader – like a chef would mix chocolate with chilli!

Create characters that YOU would like to read about. If you don't find them interesting, nobody else will!

What not to do:

- Write about your friends' deepest darkest secrets . . . unless you want to be a billy-no-mates!

- Include so-boring-we're-snoring descriptions. No one's going to be interested in what you ate for dinner last night – unless you're writing a cook book.

- Model your characters on your friends without changing their names. If you do that, then don't be surprised if someone gets their own back by putting you in a crime story!

Can You be Trusted?

Do the test and see if you are a trustworthy person.

When my friends tell me a secret:

A. I don't mean to tell anyone, it just slips out!

B. I'd sooner eat a spoonful of mustard than reveal it to anyone.

C. I tell the first person I see – you can't beat a good old gossip.

My friends:

A. Tell me EVERYTHING about themselves.

B. Know I'm not very good at keeping secrets, but like me anyway.

A. What friends?!

When it comes to promises:

A. I sometimes honestly forget that I made a promise.

B. Even holding me down and tickling me won't make me break it.

C. I don't care that I've given my word. It's just a . . . word.

I have:

A. A large group of friends and acquaintances.

B. A few really close pals. We know each other inside out.

C. I know lots of people. We talk about everything . . . and everyone.

Now work out which answer you chose most often, and read on to see if people can trust you.

Top secret

You're incredibly sociable and have lots of friends. However, sometimes you just can't help yourself from saying more than you should!
TOP TIP: Try to be a little more discrete – your pals will love you for it.

You are the queen of discretion. When someone tells you a secret, they know it'll go no further. You always keep your promises and expect others to do the same.
TOP TIP: Don't forget to put yourself first sometimes.

People love you because you've always got the latest gossip. However, few people reveal their secrets to you because you pass them on faster than they can say "Don't tell anyone!"
TOP TIP: A little less gossiping will make you a better friend.

Comet and Hurricane

It was morning, and Mia's phone rang.

"Hi, it's Karen from school!" a voice said from the other end of the line.

"Hello!" Mia greeted her cheerfully.

"I've got a huge favour to ask! I'm going on holiday tomorrow with my parents and I can't find anyone to take care of my animals, Comet and Hurricane . . ."

A loud neighing over the line interrupted her.

"Calm down, Comet!" Karen cried. "Stop making so much noise!"

"Oh!" thought Mia. "I think I hear horses! And Comet's a great name for a racer..."

"Mia, I know you love animals," Karen said, "and that's why I'm asking. Could I leave them with you? Just for a few days?"

"Two new horses..." Mia thought. "Of course!" she cried.

There was neighing again on the line.

"Comet sounds happy," Mia said.

"Sure, and Hurricane too!" Karen said. "So I'll bring them in the evening! Thanks! I've got to go, my battery is low . . ." Then there was silence on the line.

"But where will I keep them?" Mia thought.

They usually had places at the Whitehorse Stables but today all the stalls were taken!

Hello

Half an hour later, all the friends – Mia, Olivia, Andrea, Emma and Stephanie – were waiting at the stables. They gazed thoughtfully at the horses in the stalls.

"If I'm counting correctly," Emma said, "there are just as many horses here as there are stalls. So it doesn't look like there's room for Lightning and Tornado."

"Comet and Hurricane," Mia corrected her. "But you're right – there isn't any room left here."

"There's only one solution," said Olivia. "Since there aren't any more stables in Heartlake . . . we'll have to build our own!"

The other girls looked at her in surprise. "All by ourselves?" asked Emma.

"What's the problem?" Olivia replied. "We don't need to build a five-star hotel, just a simple stable for two horses. That's all!"

Stephanie made some quick calculations. "What are we all standing around for?" she asked. "We should have started forty minutes ago, if we want to finish in time."

"So let's get to work!" cried Mia.

So let's get to work!

An hour later, preparations were well underway. Andrea popped over to Whitehorse Stables to borrow everything they needed to make the horses comfortable during their stay.

Olivia got busy sketching a design for the horses' new home.

"We only need one!" laughed Stephanie, looking over her friend's shoulder at the dozens of different designs Olivia had come up with.

"I think I got a bit carried away!" Olivia grinned.

"Oh well, at least we've got extras."

Emma returned from home carrying armfuls of bunting and some gorgeous paper pompoms. "We can use them to decorate the stables," she said excitedly. "It'll look really pretty."

Just then Mia appeared with two horses, Robin and Niki, each pulling a cart behind them. The first was full of planks of wood, the second with hay and feed.

"Hooray!" cheered Stephanie. "Now we can really get started."

The new stables slowly rose. Stephanie, Olivia and Andrea nailed the boards together. Mia prepared the hay for the horses' beds and made a watering trough. Emma carefully unravelled the bunting and trimmed the pompoms.

"We should be done on time!" Stephanie smiled happily, stepping back to survey their work. "We just need to put on the roof."

Suddenly there was a loud knocking sound.

"What's that?" said Stephanie.

"It sounds like somebody's inside knocking," said Andrea, looking around.

"It's me!" The girls heard Olivia's voice. But there was no sign of her.

"Where are you?" shouted Stephanie.

"Inside the stable," Olivia shouted back. "The door seems to have disappeared."

Stephanie, Mia, Andrea and Emma stared at the stable. It was true. The door to the stable had been covered up with board.

"Oh no," Mia said shamefacedly. "That was me. I think I was holding the design upside down. "

Fortunately, the girls managed to pull the boards back off and let Olivia out.

Finally, the last nail was in place. The girls stepped back to admire their work. The stables looked lovely: the hay was arranged neatly, the blankets were hung on the door and the bunting swayed gently in the evening breeze.

"Girls . . ." Mia began. "Don't you think, perhaps, the stables are, um, a little, bit, well . . ."

"Small," finished Olivia.

The girls fell silent. There was no doubt that the stables looked absolutely gorgeous, but it was definitely too small to hold two horses.

"What are we going to do?" asked Mia.

"Perhaps we could build them some bunk beds?" suggested Andrea.

She didn't hear the reply, because suddenly a car horn sounded.

"Mia, there you are!" shouted Karen, jumping out of the car.

"Hi, Karen," Mia smiled nervously. "Um, there might be a little bit of a problem."

Karen didn't answer. She was too busy pulling a small puppy and a cage with a parrot inside out of the car.

"I'd like you to meet my pets," she said. "Hurricane and Comet."

The girls froze.

"Meow!" squawked the parrot.

Karen laughed.

"Comet is amazing," she explained. "She can imitate all sorts of different animals."

"Like a horse . . ." Mia said slowly, remembering the telephone conversation that morning.

"So, what's the problem?" Karen asked Mia.

"Oh, nothing," Mia said quickly, winking at the other girls. "Just that they're so cute, I might have trouble giving them back."

"Neigh!" squawked the parrot, and the girls burst out laughing.

Which Pet Suits You?

The friends from Heartlake City love all animals. What about you? Take this quiz to find out which animal you're most suited to.

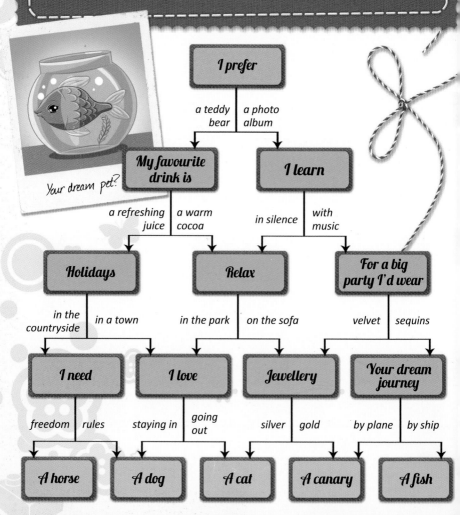

Your dream pet?

I prefer

a teddy bear → **My favourite drink is**

a photo album → **I learn**

My favourite drink is
- a refreshing juice
- a warm cocoa

I learn
- in silence
- with music

Holidays
- in the countryside
- in a town

Relax
- in the park
- on the sofa

For a big party I'd wear
- velvet
- sequins

I need
- freedom → **A horse**
- rules → **A dog**

I love
- staying in → **A dog**
- going out → **A cat**

Jewellery
- silver → **A cat**
- gold → **A canary**

Your dream journey
- by plane → **A canary**
- by ship → **A fish**

A horse   You're fond of nature, just like Mia. A horse would suit you down to the ground because you like your freedom and enjoy the outdoor life. Maybe it's time for you to visit your local stable?

A dog   You are hard-working and responsible, just like Stephanie. You like exercise and outdoor activities, making you the perfect dog owner! Not only will you have a great time together, but you'll get a new friend into the bargain too!

A cat   Rules and regulations are not for you. You like your independence and want to be free to explore your interests, just like Olivia. The perfect pet for you is a cat because it comes and goes as it pleases, but also needs to be cuddled and stroked.

A canary   Music fills almost every part of your life, just like it does Andrea's. And wouldn't it be awesome to have a pet who shared your passion? Your best choice would be a canary who will sing especially for you. Who knows, maybe one day you'll perform together!

A fish   You're not a natural with animals – cats, hedgehogs, they're all the same to you! However, you do love pretty trinkets, just like Emma does. A colourful fish would be perfect for you. If nothing else, it'll make a shiny new decoration for your room!

A Little Kingdom

There's nothing quite like having your own space. So whether your room is big or small, shared or all your own, follow Emma's tips to make your nook extra cosy for you and your pet.

🐾 Something soft

Do you have a bed or sofa in your special space? Soft cushions decorated in your favourite patterns will make your room seem warm and comfortable. If you have a dog or cat, remember that they should also have their own beds – suitable for their size.

🐾 Something individual

A photo frame, a holiday souvenir or a hand-made box for bits and pieces will make your nook look special and unique. Your pet probably won't have a collection of friends' postcards to put up, so perhaps try decorating their bed with a colourful blanket or their name.

🐾 Something cherished

We all have special things we like to surround ourselves with. Even just a few of these scattered about your space will make it feel more 'yours'. You can also take care of your four-legged friend by decorating their bed with their favourite toys.

🐾 Something delicious

It's fun to chill out in your nook! And it's even better when you've got a snack, so make sure you remember to leave space for a cup and plate. Don't forget about your pet either – they like to eat too!

🐾 Something shiny

So now your room is looking super cosy. Now put up a picture of your favourite pop star or cute animal. Make sure you keep your little kingdom spotless, so you and your pet can really enjoy it.

What's Your Friendship Role?

Olivia, Andrea, Emma, Mia and Stephanie know that by combining their strengths they can move mountains. Together with your pals, find out what role each of you has in your friendship group.

In a shopping mall:
A) I know exactly where I'm going
B) I can't wait to leave
C) I rush to the bookstore
D) I meet my friends at a coffee shop
E) I help my pals with their shopping

What suits me best is:
A) A multifunctional watch
B) A set of screwdrivers
C) A camera
D) A colourful MP3 player
E) A lip gloss

In a school play:
A) I'm the director
B) I paint the scenery
C) I prepare the music
D) I play the lead
E) I design the costumes

My doodles often look like:
A) ⭐ B) 🦋 C) ❤ D) 🎵 E) 🍀

Friends

 ### A leader

You're great at keeping everyone busy, but don't get so caught up in planning that you forget to pitch in yourself. Your friends will thank you for helping out!

 ### A handy girl

You can always be relied on when anything needs to be moved, built or repaired. Your friends appreciate it and secretly admire your ability to cope with difficult situations.

A thinker

Complicated calculations? A new invention? It's a piece of cake for you! You are very smart so you can improve almost everything. All you need is a pencil, a piece of paper and . . . a few seconds to think.

 ### A star

Is singing your thing? Or maybe you have an acting talent? Thanks to your skills you not only make friends easily but also lift your pals' mood and make life more colourful.

A stylist

You're best at tasks that make the most of your artistic talents. You can design and make fantastic outfits, do beautiful make-up and create super-cute hairstyles too!

Magic Mia

The friends met up in the tree house, as they did every Friday after school.

"Where's Mia?" Emma asked as she climbed the ladder.

"She hasn't turned up, again," replied Andrea, shuffling out of Emma's way.

"She hasn't had any time for us lately," Stephanie added sadly. "What's up with her?"

"I don't know," Andrea said gloomily. "She could at least have popped in to say hello."

The girls did their best to enjoy themselves. It was a lovely afternoon, and they had two whole days off school ahead of them, but it just wasn't the same without Mia. The friends had hardly seen her all week. Every night, as soon as the bell rang, Mia had picked up her bag and rushed off. And instead of joining them at break times like she ususally did, Mia had just waved a distracted hello, before hurrying off. It wasn't like her and the friends were worried.

Suddenly all of the friends' phones beeped at the same time.

"I've got a text from Mia," Olivia exclaimed.

"Me too!" said Emma.

"And me," added Andrea.

"Saturday. Six p.m. My place," Stephanie read out loud. "What's that all about?"

"No idea," Emma replied, staring at the message.

"Why is she being so mysterious?" asked Andrea.

"I guess we'll find out tomorrow," said Olivia.

At 6 p.m. sharp the next day, Stephanie, Olivia, Emma and Andrea were waiting in front of Mia's house. They couldn't wait to find out why Mia had been acting so strangely.

Olivia knocked on the door. No one answered. Instead, the door opened slowly by itself. The girls looked at each other before stepping gingerly inside.

"Hey!" Olivia cried. "What's this? There's some kind of wire here!"

And there was indeed a fishing line tied to the door handle. The other end seemed to be somewhere inside the house . . .

"Mia!" shouted Andrea. "Are you here?"

No one answered. The girls stepped forward cautiously, peering into each room. When they entered the dining room, they got scared: all of the windows were covered and there was no light.

"Mia?" Stephanie called. "Where are you?"

They heard a voice from the other end of the room: "Please welcome the amazing Magic Mia! Mistress of mystery and illusion!"

A spotlight beamed from behind the girls, illuminating the curtain. Suddenly Mia entered the circle of light, leaving her friends dumbstruck.

"What are you wearing?" Emma stammered.

Mia twirled happily. She wore a gleaming black tailcoat, a shiny waistcoat and a red cape. On her head she wore a huge top hat, and in her hands she held a short black-and-white wand.

"Fantastic, don't you think?" Mia smiled broadly. "I bought everything at a charity shop."

Mia grinned at her friends.

"This is my magician's set," Mia said, gesturing at a small table covered with a tablecloth in a pattern of gold stars, and a matching wardrobe behind her. "I hope you're ready for a magical evening!"

The girls stared at her open-mouthed.

"It's really cool!" Mia exclaimed. "I've been practising non-stop! You're going to love it!"

"Was that bit of wire by the door part of it?" asked Olivia.

"Oh," Mia said. "Um, yes. You weren't supposed to notice the wire. Never mind, I've mastered the other tricks perfectly."

She smiled at her friends. "Now, sit down, relax and enjoy the show!"

The girls obediently sat down on chairs that Mia had arranged in front of the 'stage'. Mia cleared her throat and extended her arms towards the audience.

"As you can see, ladies and gentlemen. Er, I mean ladies and um, ladies, my sleeves are completely empty . . ." Before she could finish some playing cards slipped out of her sleeve.

"Oh no!" exclaimed Mia, trying to catch the cards. "Apologies. Some small technical problems." She pulled her sleeve back down, then reached up and took off her top hat. "Let's begin with something a little easier."

The girls clapped loudly as Mia began pulling several brightly coloured handkerchiefs out of the hat. Suddenly something snapped.

"Oops," Mia exclaimed. "Um, that wasn't meant to happen."
Mia pulled hard on the handkerchiefs, but they didn't move.

"And so . . . moving on to our next trick!' Mia pushed the
hat back on her head, with a coloured string still sticking
out of it.

Trick after trick continued to go wrong.

Other tricks also weren't fully successful, but Mia did her
best. A hidden bouquet of flowers fell out of the leg of her
trousers when she leaned over to pick up some juggling balls
she had dropped. Then Mia got her cape caught in the door to
the 'disappearing cabinet', almost knocking over the whole
wardrobe with her inside. Even the secret compartment in the
wand didn't want to open.

"This time nothing can go wrong," Mia joked as she shuffled
a deck of cards.

Each girl drew a card. Mia asked Stephanie: "Do you hold
the ace of hearts?"

Stephanie glanced at her hand.

"Yes!" she exclaimed, revealing the card. "How did
you know?"

Mia was just as surprised herself, and stammered, "I haven't the foggiest . . . I mean, it's magic! Ta-daaa!"

When the show was over, Mia's friends walked home silently. They were all thinking of Mia's latest, somewhat unfortunate passion.

"But that last trick was great," said Emma. "Wasn't it, Stephanie? I'm curious how Mia knew what card you had?"

"I helped her a little," Stephanie admitted.

"What?!" cried Olivia and Andrea, and Emma almost fell over.

Stephanie sighed.

"I had to. All the tricks were going so terribly wrong. After the first trick, there were lots of cards lying on the floor. I picked one up. It just happened to be the ace of hearts."

"But then Mia guessed which card you drew?" Emma asked, fixing her hair band. "It was the ace of hearts, right?"

"Wrong," Stephanie replied.

"But we saw it!" Andrea added. "An ace with a red heart!"

"In fact I drew a nine of spades from the deck," Stephanie admitted. "But then I switched the cards."

The girls looked at each other.

Olivia was the first to speak. "You did the right thing," she said. "Mia really wants to become a magician."

"Yeah," Andrea added. "And she won't give us a moment's peace until she does! Who knows what else she's got up her sleeve. Apart from more cards. Ha, ha."

"So we need to help her," Olivia decided. "We'll secretly improve the tricks until the show is perfect. It's easy, or at least we can figure it out!"

It's magic!

The girls kept walking, discussing the details of their secret plan.

There were more magic shows over the next few days, and they steadily improved. More and more tricks worked, and Mia was beaming with joy. When Mia wasn't looking, Olivia secretly oiled all the hinges and adjusted the springs of the 'magic set'. "She also invented a few gadgets of her own and hid them in Mia's tailcoat. The other girls oohed and aahed at the tricks, even when they knew that something hadn't gone quite right.

But when the watch borrowed from Andrea mysteriously disappeared from the table (the girls had hidden a super-strong magnet under Olivia's chair), the magician rubbed her eyes in disbelief.

"Girls, I need to tell you something," Mia announced. "You've probably all noticed that I've made huge progress in the last few days. I know I've practised a lot, but my magician's handbook says it's simply impossible to learn so many tricks in such a short time. There's only one possible explanation . . ." Her voice trailed off.

The other girls froze.

"She knows!" Andrea whispered to Emma, who was sitting next to her.

Mia spoke slowly. "I think I am . . . a magic genius!"

Her friends looked at one another stunned.

"Because," Mia explained with growing conviction, "if it is impossible to do such hard tricks so fast, I must have real talent! And that's not all!"

The girls were speechless.

"I've signed up to take part in the Summer Festival tomorrow! It's going to be broadcast on TV. Everyone will be able to watch me work my magic. How cool is that?"

Silence fell. Then Olivia spoke.

"Um, yes, really cool," she murmured. The other girls slowly nodded their heads.

"So what do we do now?" Emma asked. The four of them had gone to the café to discuss Mia's announcement.

"We can't tell Mia she's no good at magic," Stephanie insisted. "She'll be crushed."

"But we can't let her go on TV!" Olivia exclaimed. "We won't be on stage, so how can we help her?!"

"What can we do?!" Emma fretted. She squeezed a hairpin so much that it shot under the next table. "We've got to tell her the truth. Mia has to withdraw from the festival!"

"If we tell Mia the truth she'll never talk to us again," Stephanie pointed out.

"Well, it would be a little quieter," Andrea tried to joke, but the other girls shot her down with their eyes.

"We have to confess," Olivia argued. "Otherwise Mia will end up looking stupid. And it'll be our fault."

"I agree with Olivia," Andrea admitted.

"Me too," Emma said.

"One thing's for sure," Stephanie sighed. "I don't think she's going to like it."

The next day, the friends met at the Summer Festival. Despite their best efforts, they hadn't been able to get hold of Mia all morning and she was due on stage any moment.

"There she is!" cried Olivia, as Mia walked towards the stage, holding her magician's hat in place.

"Where have you been?" Emma cried. "We've been ringing you all morning."

"I've been getting ready of course," said Mia. "I'm about to go on TV."

Andrea looked at the others and took a deep breath.

"Mia," she began. "We've got something to tell you . . ."

"It'll have to wait until after the show," said Mia. "I'm on!"

She strode on to the stage, waving happily at the audience.

"I can't bear to watch," Stephanie mumbled, putting her hands over her eyes.

On stage, Mia bowed at the audience, then took off her hat with a flourish. From out of the hat she pulled a rabbit! As the audience applauded, birds flew out of her sleeves.

"Stephanie, look!" Andrea nudged.

"Hey!" cried Emma. "She didn't do those tricks before!"

In every one of Mia's tricks, animals played some role. Rabbits jumped, scattering colourful handkerchiefs everywhere, parrots disappeared in the top hat or the cabinet and then flew out from behind the curtain. Puppies shuffled cards with their noses. And each trick was more enjoyable than the last. The audience was delighted.

When the show ended, the girls ran up to Mia.

"Why didn't you tell us?" Andrea asked.

"That I was using animals in my act?" laughed Mia. "It was an obvious thing to do. I can manage animals much better than cards!"

"But . . . but . . ." stuttered Emma.

Mia smiled at her friends.

"I'll never be talented at ordinary tricks. But I think you all know that, don't you."

The other girls turned red.

Magician :)

"I knew all along that you were secretly helping me."

"You're not mad at us."

"Of course not!" Mia giggled. "You were trying to do the right thing. But I had you going, didn't I?" She nudged Emma.

"Just a little," breathed Olivia. "I've never been so worried!"

"You know what I think is really magic?" asked Mia, pulling her friends into a hug. "Having such good friends."

Hocus Pocus

Mia is much better at teaching animals tricks than using a magic wand. But she has managed to learn some magic. Use these simple tricks to amaze your friends . . .

A magic touch

The secret . . .
The secret to this trick is to touch each coin to check its temperature. The coin chosen by the volunteer will be warmer.

This trick is about identifying the coin chosen by a volunteer from the audience while you're blindfolded.

1. Put three identical coins on the table and ask somebody from the audience to cover your eyes with a piece of cloth.

2. Choose a volunteer. Ask him to take a coin, count to 20 and put it back.

3. Touch each coin and with a dramatic gesture, pick up the right one and then show it to the audience.

Top tip
If you can't sense which coin is warmest after just one touch, pick up each coin and pretend to weigh it in your hand, to give yourself more time.

Magic eggs!

In this trick you make two identical eggs behave in completely different ways. One will sink in a glass of water and the other will be floating on the surface.

Before the trick

Dissolve some salt in a glass of warm water. Place the glass next to the second glass filled with ordinary water. Remember which is which. Then place some eggs in a bowl.

1. Ask a volunteer to choose two eggs from the bowl. Then announce in a mysterious voice which egg will sink and which will stay on the surface.

2. Put the eggs into the glasses very carefully and... wait for the applause.

The secret . . .

The glasses look the same but one is filled with salt solution which makes the egg float on the surface.

Friendship Test

The girls from Heartlake City are really good friends –
they not only have fun together but can also rely on
themselves. And what kind of friend are you?
Find out with this fun friendship test!

What do you do when . . .

Your friend is sick.
- I visit her and try to cheer her up. ✹✹✹
- I call her and tell her what a good time I'm having
  with other girls. ✹
- I tell her about what we've been doing during lessons so
  that she can catch up at home. ✹✹

**When your friend is sitting next to you and you have only one
chocolate bar:**
- I give it to my friend, she likes it as much as I do. ✹✹
- I eat it secretly. ✹
- I divide it in half and share it. ✹✹✹

**Your friend wants to take part in a school karaoke contest but
she can't sing.**
- I do my best to talk her out of it. ✹✹
- I have fun singing along with her. ✹✹✹
- I encourage her to take part – it'll give me a
  good laugh. ✹

Your friend is taking part in the same race as you.
- I trip her up before the finishing line. ✳
- I let her win. ✳✳
- I give her my hand and we cross the finishing line together. ✳✳✳

When your friend shares her biggest secret with you.
- I do the same. ✳✳
- I promise to keep it that way. ✳✳✳
- I'm happy – now I'll have something new to tell everyone. ✳

From 5 to 7 ✳

Hmmm, friendship just isn't your strong point. But not to worry, just try to pay a bit more attention to the needs of others and you'll soon become ideal friend material.

From 8 to 11 ✳

You're very helpful, which attracts people to you. You treasure your friends, and will go to the ends of the earth for them. Just don't forget to think of yourself sometimes too!

From 12 to 15 ✳

Having you as a friend is like winning a jackpot prize. You are a very reliable person. You never forget about your friends, you always share everything with them and they do the same.

Friends

Hidden Talents

Not sure what you're good at? Think you're a totally talent-free zone? You couldn't be more wrong! Here are Andrea and Emma's top talent-finding tips . . .

• Think about what you love to do. What you enjoy the most is often what you're best at.

• Talent doesn't just include musical, acting or artistic skills. Stephanie is a great planner and Mia has a natural connection with animals. Maybe you have a unique gift too, just like them?

• Talent alone is not enough. Once you've found your special ability you need to keep working on it. That's all part of the fun!

• Take a moment to think about how you'd end each of these sentences – they might provide clues to your hidden talent. If it helps, write your answers on a piece of paper and use them as a guide . . .

I'm most interested in . . .

I can't stop thinking about . . .

I love chatting about . . .

I love learning about . . .

When I have free time, I enjoy . . .

Look out for this other fab LEGO® Friends book!

It's the day of the big Creativity Festival in Heartlake City, and the girls can't wait to do their bit – especially Olivia, who has a very special role to play.

Read the story, complete the activities and play along with your very own super-cute LEGO kitten mini-set.